P9-DFB-839

All Things Bright and Beautiful

ISBN-13: 978-0-8249-5676-9

Published by WorthyKids/Ideals
An imprint of Worthy Publishing Group
A division of Worthy Media, Inc.
Nashville, Tennessee

Designed by Georgina Chidlow
Printed and bound in China

RRD-SZ_Apr16_2

Library of Congress Cataloging-in-Publication Data

Names: Alexander, Cecil Frances, 1818-1895 author. | Hudson, Katy, illustrator.
Title: All things bright and beautiful / Cecil Frances Alexander, art by Katy Hudson.
Description: Nashville, Tennessee : WorthyKids/Ideals, [2016] | Includes bibliographical references and index.
Identifiers: LCCN 2015033396 | ISBN 9780824956769 (hardback)
Subjects: LCSH: Hymns, English—Juvenile literature. | Children's poetry, English. | Hymns, English—Texts. | Nature—Religious aspects—Christianity—Juvenile literature. | Creation—Juvenile literature. | Praise of God—Juvenile literature. | BISAC: JUVENILE FICTION / Religious / Christian / General.
Classification: LCC BV353 .A44 2016 | DDC 264/.23—dc23
LC record available at http://lccn.loc.gov/2015033396

For Grandma, Granddad Ron,
Granddad Andy, and Nan.
—K.H.

All Things Bright and Beautiful

Written by
Cecil Frances Alexander
Illustrated by
Katy Hudson

WorthyKids
ideals™
Nashville, Tennessee

All things bright and beautiful,

All creatures great and small,

All things wise and wonderful:
The Lord God made them all.

Each little flower that opens,
Each little bird that sings,

He made their glowing colors,
He made their tiny wings.

The purple-headed mountain,
The river running by,

The sunset and the morning
That brightens up the sky,

The cold wind in the winter,
The pleasant summer sun,

The ripe fruits in the garden:
He made them, every one.

The tall trees in the greenwood,
The meadows where we play,

The rushes by the water
We gather every day:

He gave us eyes to see them,
And lips that we might tell

How great is God Almighty,
Who has made all things well.

All things bright and beautiful,
All creatures great and small,

All things wise and wonderful:
The Lord God made them all.

In the beginning God created the heaven and the earth. . . .
And God saw every thing that he had made, and, behold, it was very good.

— Genesis 1:1, 31a (KJV)